To Síobhán

First published in Great Britain 2001
by Egmont Children's Books Limited
a division of Egmont Holding Limited
239 Kensington High Street, London W8 6SA

Text and illustrations copyright © Mary Murphy 2001
Mary Murphy has asserted her moral rights
Design by Phil Powell. Flowers by Phil Powell & Paul Staples
0 7497 4407 3

A CIP catalogue record for this title is available from the British Library

Printed in Hong Kong

1 2 3 4 5 6 7 8 9 10

Koala
and the
Flower

Mary Murphy

EGMONT CHILDREN'S BOOKS

Badger and Raccoon see things in black and white. They are always sure that they are always right. Little grey Koala isn't sure about many things. She asks lots of questions.

Badger knows that Badger is right.

Raccoon knows that Raccoon is right.

And they
both know
that they know
much more than Koala.

One day, Koala goes for a walk.

She goes slowly, looking at things from all sides.

She finds something new. It is a yellow flower.

Koala has never

seen a yellow

flower before,

except in a picture.

You're lovely!

Koala runs all the way home...

"Guess what I saw!" she says.
"A yellow flower! Come and see!"

But Badger and Raccoon are too busy.

Koala picks the flower
and brings it home.

"**Where** do flowers come from?" she asks.

Badger and Raccoon are sure they know.

Koala puts the flower in a jar so that she can look at it.

She doesn't know that flowers need water.

The flower dies.

"Poor flower!" says Koala.

"I should have left you where you were."

MAKING FLOWERS (by Raccoon)

1. "Raccoon, how do we get flowers?"

"Easy! We make them from paper"

Raccoon shows Koala how to make flowers.

2. "That's right"

They fetch paper and wire and string and glue.

3. They cut and twist and tie and stick.

4. "Poor Koala"

But it doesn't turn out right. "You did it wrong," says Raccoon.

MAKING FLOWERS (by Badger)

Koala goes for another walk with some flower biscuits in her backpack.

She walks and walks and walks. She goes further than she

has ever gone before.

She meets a little grey donkey. (He looks very big to Koala.) Koala tells him about her flower.

"I don't know how to make flowers," says Donkey.

"But there is a place I go when I want to find out things."

Koala didn't know there were so many books in the world. She didn't know there were so many animals trying to find out things. She didn't know that most animals know that they don't know everything.

"This is great!" she says.

Koala goes home with a backpack full of books.

She reads…

…and reads.

Koala buys some seeds.

"Now I can make some flowers," she says.

She shakes seeds from her own beloved flower too.

Badger and Raccoon snigger. They laugh when she

digs a patch in a sunny part of the garden.

They guffaw when she puts the seeds on the ground and covers them with earth.

They roll about when she sprinkles water on the seeds. But Koala doesn't care.

Koala reads her library books and waits for her seeds to grow. Sometimes the sun shines…

And sometimes clouds bring rain.

After a few days, little green spikes poke out of the earth. Koala tends the flower patch. She carries snails away.

She waters the earth. Soon little buds appear on top of the little green spikes. Time goes by and…

...this is what happens.

"Come and see!" says Koala to Badger and Raccoon.

"Well done!" says Badger. "Just what I expected."

"Me too!" says Raccoon. "First rate!"

"I knew it!" says Koala. "I knew it would work!"

Now Koala knows about lots of flowers, and insects, and colours.

"It's still like magic," she says…

Thank you, Koala!

"...at least that's what I think!"

A Story for Hippo
by Simon Puttock and Alison Bartlett
0 7497 4022 1

Mr Wolf's Pancakes by Jan Fearnley
0 7497 3559 7

Cat's Colours by Jane Cabrera
0 7497 3120 6

Dog's Day by Jane Cabrera
0 7497 4392 1

I wish I were a dog by Lydia Monks
0 7497 3803 0

The Three Little Wolves and the Big Bad Pig
by Eugene Trivizas and Helen Oxenbury
0 7497 2505 2

And they're all only £4.99